Six
by
Seuss

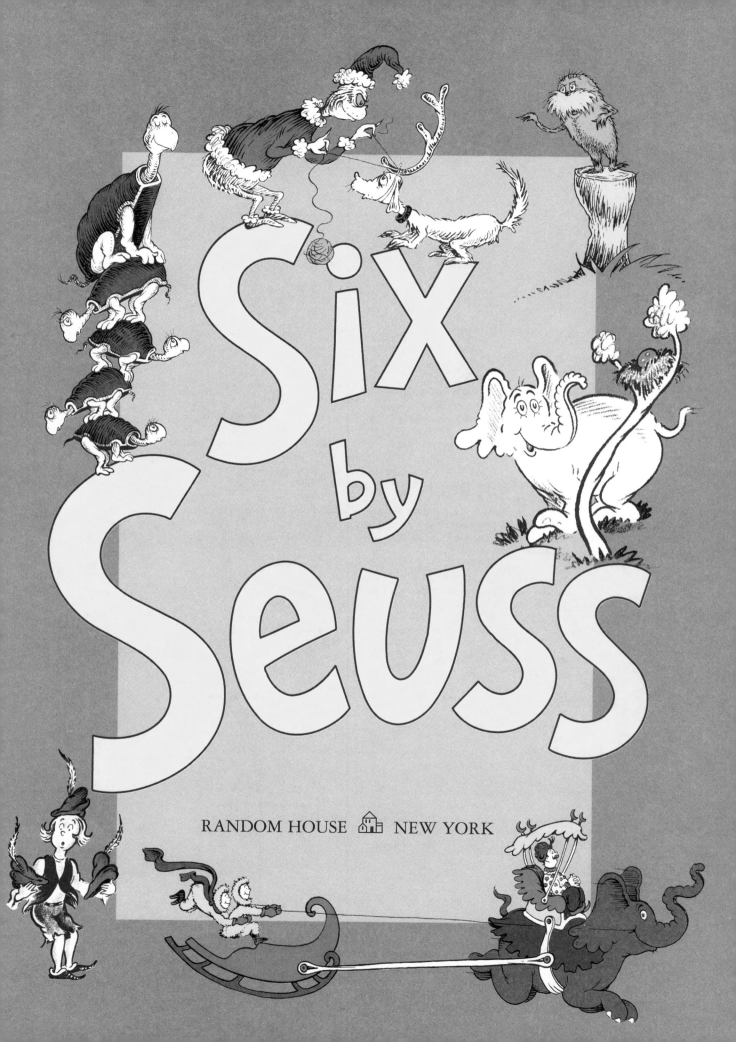

Six by Seuss

RANDOM HOUSE 🏠 NEW YORK

Compilation TM & © 1991 by Dr. Seuss Enterprises, L.P.
Introduction copyright © 1991 by Clifton Fadiman
The following titles by Dr. Seuss were originally published by Random House Children's Books,
a division of Random House, Inc., as follows:
And to Think That I Saw It on Mulberry Street TM & © 1937, renewed 1964 by Dr. Seuss Enterprises, L.P.
The 500 Hats of Bartholomew Cubbins TM & © 1938, renewed 1965 by Dr. Seuss Enterprises, L.P.
Horton Hatches the Egg TM & © 1940, renewed 1968 by Dr. Seuss Enterprises, L.P.
Yertle the Turtle and Other Stories TM & © 1950, 1951, 1958, renewed 1977, 1979, 1986
by Dr. Seuss Enterprises, L.P.
How the Grinch Stole Christmas! TM & © 1957, renewed 1985 by Dr. Seuss Enterprises, L.P.
The Lorax ® and © 1971, renewed 1999 by Dr. Seuss Enterprises, L.P.
This compilation was originally published in 1991 by Random House Children's Books,
a division of Random House, Inc.

Published in the United States by Random House Children's Books,
a division of Random House, Inc., New York.

RANDOM HOUSE and colophon are registered trademarks of Random House, Inc.

www.randomhouse.com/kids
www.seussville.com

Educators and librarians, for a variety of teaching tools, visit us at www.randomhouse.com/teachers

Library of Congress Cataloging-in-Publication Data
Seuss, Dr.
[Selections. 1991]
Six by Seuss : a treasury of Dr. Seuss classics.
   p. cm.
SUMMARY: An anthology of six stories by Dr. Seuss, including "And to Think That I Saw It
on Mulberry Street," "The 500 Hats of Bartholomew Cubbins," "Horton Hatches the Egg,"
"How the Grinch Stole Christmas!," "The Lorax," and "Yertle the Turtle."
ISBN: 978-0-679-82148-9 (trade)
1. Children's stories, American.   [1. Stories in rhyme.]
I. Title.
PZ8.3.G276Si 1991 91-6311 [E]—dc20

Printed in the United States of America   20 19 18 17 16 15 14 13

Contents

Introduction

*As Clifton Fadiman wrote in his January 1991 introduction
to* Six by Seuss *. . .*

The Geisels (Ted was then in his early thirties) were returning from
Europe on the *Kungsholm.* In time to the stroke of the ship's engines, he
found himself mumbling:

> *And that is a story that no one can beat,*
> *And to think that I saw it on Mulberry Street.*

After a reasonable number of mumbles, Helen Geisel, feeling that enough
was enough, suggested to her cartoonist husband that he work up an illustrated children's book in which this couplet might be happily buried.
He did so. According to one report, twenty-seven publishers rejected it;
according to another, forty-three. Their reasons were irrefutable: Verse
didn't sell; Fantasy didn't sell; *Mulberry Street* would improve neither the
child's character nor his or her earning capacity. But the twenty-eighth,
or the forty-fourth, publisher had no head for business. He just liked
Mulberry Street.

Since 1937 Dr. Seuss, as Ted Geisel is universally known, has added
forty-five prescriptions to his original Rx. For over fifty-four years the
good doctor has paid untold millions of house calls to welcoming children
and their grateful parents. With sales upwards of 200 million, he has
become part of the environment, a kind of public utility. Nothing in
the history of books for children comes within hailing distance of this
phenomenon.

Dr. Seuss, who happens to be childless, says laconically, "You make 'em—I amuse 'em." As we do, he does. Well, I am partly responsible for three children. I have watched them break into hoots, howls, and hurricanes of laughter over *On Beyond Zebra!* (our family favorite) or *Thidwick the Big-Hearted Moose* or any of the six prime exhibits here collected. Our youngsters waived self-improvement. All they wanted was more Seuss.

But if the doctor offered only hilarity, writers of introductions would wither on the word processor. There had better be more to it than that.

Only a few creative mutations interrupt the evolution of children's books. We think at once, among others, of *Alice in Wonderland* (1865), *Little Women* (1868–69), *Where the Wild Things Are* (1963). Each furnished a key to unlock a room in the child's imagination that others had not explored. *Mulberry Street* and *The Cat in the Hat* (1957) were no less revolutionary, a kind of Imagination Proclamation. With its jingly-jangly, yell-it-out-loud verse, with its aggressively visible cartoony pictures, *Mulberry Street* thumbed its nose at blandness and sentimentality, boldly asserted the right to exaggerate, and put parents in their proper place. *The Cat in the Hat* liquidated Dick and Jane forever, its 223 basic words persuading the wee beginner that reading could be fun. No American child aware of his constitutional rights can reach the age of six without absorbing *The Cat in the Hat* and one or more of Seuss's seventeen Beginner Books that have followed it.

Dr. Seuss's people (except for his little boy, who is Every Child) look a bit like comic monsters; his animals (what an alternate Barnum & Bailey's he has created!), a bit like comic people. And the odd objects that crowd his illustrations are no less animated than the animals and the people. He crosses his eyes, hooks on his patented distorting spectacles, stands on his head, and takes a good look at Aesop, Grimm, and other predecessors. But what happens is pure Seuss.

The 500 Hats uses the machinery of *The Sorcerer's Apprentice* and the traditional ploy of incremental repetition to take a swipe at royalty (Pop and Mom, of course) but with such comic energy that the little lesson is nicely submerged in a sea of laughter. Horton is admirable because he is faithful (and you should be too), but what counts is that he is and looks like the funniest and most lovable of elephants, almost in a class with Babar. The Lorax speaks for the trees, and has become something of a hero to ecologists. But his lesson impresses because of the Once-ler with his Snuvv, and the Brown Bar-ba-loots, and those suspicious Thneeds, and the whole crazy action conjured up in rhyme and picture. Like much of

Dr. Seuss's work, *Yertle the Turtle* contains solid, old-fashioned populist morality, but what the children really go for here is action whose outcome is decided by a burp. *Grinch* is a classic because youngsters today unconsciously prefer the familiar Scrooge motif to be translated into simple, vigorous, jokey language that's truly their own, part of their time and place, appealing to a sense of humor that welcomes the wild, the grotesque, even the mildly lunatic.

Year after year Dr. Seuss pumps fresh air into the world of children's books, whacking with the slapstick of comic fantasy the backside of whatever is stuffy or overinstructive or mannered or self-consciously whimsical. I suppose he is technically a writer-artist, but I don't think of him that way. I think of him as a performer and of his entire *oeuvre* (there's a word for you) as a kind of nonstop, continually varied panorama done in primary words and colors. For that reason I nominate him to receive next Christmas one of those annual awards the president hands out at the John F. Kennedy Center for the Performing Arts. Then millions of children would feel even more keenly that they have a stake in the country.

Clifton Fadiman
Captiva Island, Florida

Editor's Note: Nine months after this introduction was written, Ted Geisel died at his home in La Jolla, California, on September 24, 1991. He was eighty-seven years old. Over the course of his life, he completed sixty-one books. Three more titles—based on his notes and sketches, and illustrated by others—were published after his death. By 2007, his books have been published in at least thirty different languages.

Ted Geisel never was awarded a Kennedy Center Honor, but he was widely recognized during his lifetime. Works based on his original stories have won three Academy Awards, three Emmy Awards, and three Grammy Awards. In addition, he received three Caldecott Honors, a Peabody Award, the Laura Ingalls Wilder Medal, and a Pulitzer Prize.

Clifton Fadiman was a writer, critic, editor, and radio and television personality, and for more than fifty years he was a senior judge for the Book-of-the-Month Club. In 1993 he received a National Book Award for his "distinguished contribution to American letters." He died in 1999 on Sanibel Island, Florida.

Six
by
Seuss

And to Think That I Saw It on MULBERRY STREET

WHEN I leave home to walk to school,
Dad always says to me,
"Marco, keep your eyelids up
And see what you can see."

But when I tell him where I've been
And what I think I've seen,
He looks at me and sternly says,
"Your eyesight's much too keen.

"Stop telling such outlandish tales.
Stop turning minnows into whales."

Now, what can I say
When I get home today?

All the long way to school
And all the way back,
I've looked and I've looked
And I've kept careful track,
But all that I've noticed,
Except my own feet,
Was a horse and a wagon
On Mulberry Street.

That's nothing to tell of,
That won't do, of course . . .
Just a broken-down wagon
That's drawn by a horse.

That *can't* be my story. That's only a *start*.
I'll say that a ZEBRA was pulling that cart!
And that is a story that no one can beat,
When I say that I saw it on Mulberry Street.

Yes, the zebra is fine,
But I think it's a shame,
Such a marvelous beast
With a cart that's so tame.
The story would really be better to hear
If the driver I saw were a charioteer.
A gold and blue chariot's *something* to meet,
Rumbling like thunder down Mulberry Street!

No, it won't do at all . . .
A zebra's too small.

A reindeer is better;
He's fast and he's fleet,

And he'd look mighty smart
On old Mulberry Street.

Hold on a minute!
There's something wrong!

A reindeer hates the way it feels
To pull a thing that runs on wheels.

He'd be much happier, instead,
If he could pull a fancy sled.

Hmmmm . . . A reindeer and sleigh . . .

Say—*any*one could think of *that*,
Jack or Fred or Joe or Nat—
Say, even Jane could think of *that*.

But it isn't too late to make one little change.
A sleigh and an ELEPHANT! *There's* something strange!

I'll pick one with plenty of power and size,
A blue one with plenty of fun in his eyes.
And then, just to give him a little more tone,
Have a Rajah, with rubies, perched high on a throne.

Say! That makes a story that *no one* can beat,
When I say that I saw it on Mulberry Street.

But now I don't know . . .
It still doesn't seem right.

An elephant pulling a thing that's so light
Would whip it around in the air like a kite.

But he'd look simply grand
With a great big brass band!

A band that's so good should have someone to hear it,
But it's going so fast that it's hard to keep near it.
I'll put on a trailer! I know they won't mind
If a man sits and listens while hitched on behind.

But now is it fair? Is it fair what I've done?
I'll bet those wagons weigh more than a ton.
That's really too heavy a load for *one* beast;
I'll give him some helpers. He needs two, at least.

But now what worries me is this . .
Mulberry Street runs into Bliss.

30

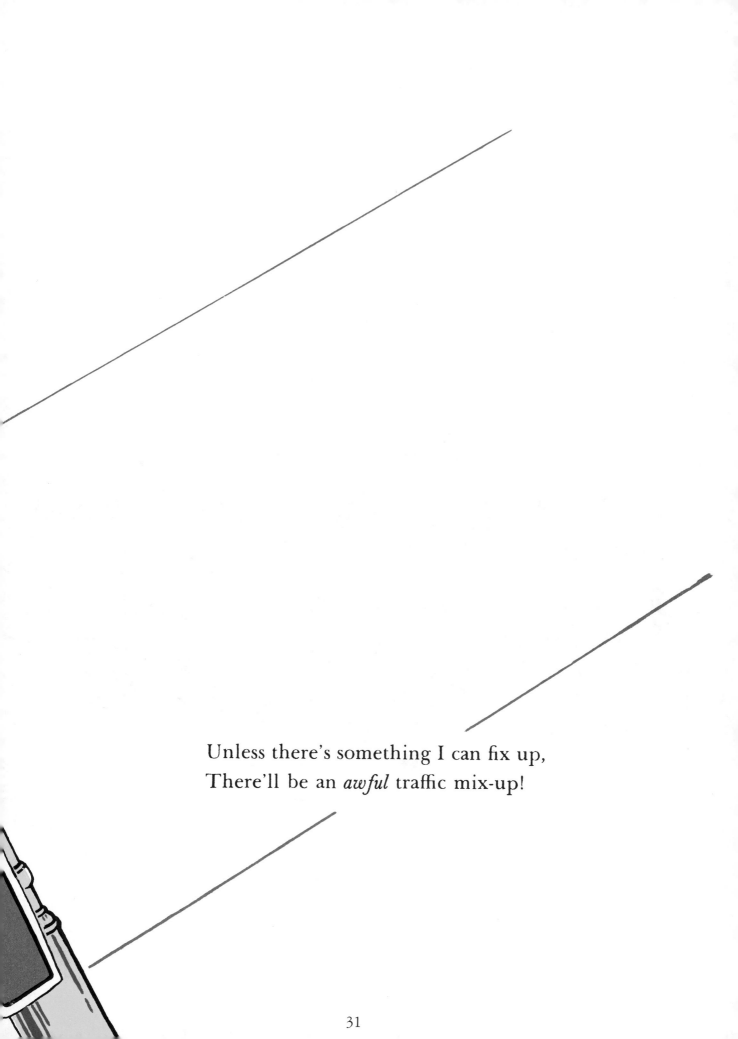

Unless there's something I can fix up,
There'll be an *awful* traffic mix-up!

It takes Police to do the trick,
To guide them through where traffic's thick —
It takes Police to do the trick.

They'll never crash now. They'll race at top speed
With Sergeant Mulvaney, himself, in the lead.

The Mayor is there
And he thinks it is grand,
And he raises his hat
As they dash by the stand.

The Mayor is there
And the Aldermen too,
All waving big banners
Of red, white and blue.

And that is a story that NO ONE can beat
When I say that I saw it on Mulberry Street!

With a roar of its motor an airplane appears
And dumps out confetti while everyone cheers.

And that makes a story that's really not bad!
But it still could be better. Suppose that I add . . . .

. . . A Chinese man
Who eats with sticks. . . .

A big Magician
Doing tricks . . .

A ten-foot beard
That needs a comb. . . .

No time for more,
I'm almost home.

I swung 'round the corner
And dashed through the gate,
I ran up the steps
And I felt simply GREAT!

FOR I HAD A STORY THAT **NO ONE** COULD BEAT!
AND TO THINK THAT I SAW IT ON MULBERRY STREET!

But Dad said quite calmly,
"Just draw up your stool
And tell me the sights
On the way home from school."

There was so much to tell, I JUST COULDN'T BEGIN!
Dad looked at me sharply and pulled at his chin.
He frowned at me sternly from there in his seat,
"Was there nothing to look at . . . no people to greet?
Did *nothing* excite you or make your heart beat?"

"Nothing," I said, growing red as a beet,
"But a plain horse and wagon on Mulberry Street."

The 500 HATS of Bartholomew Cubbins

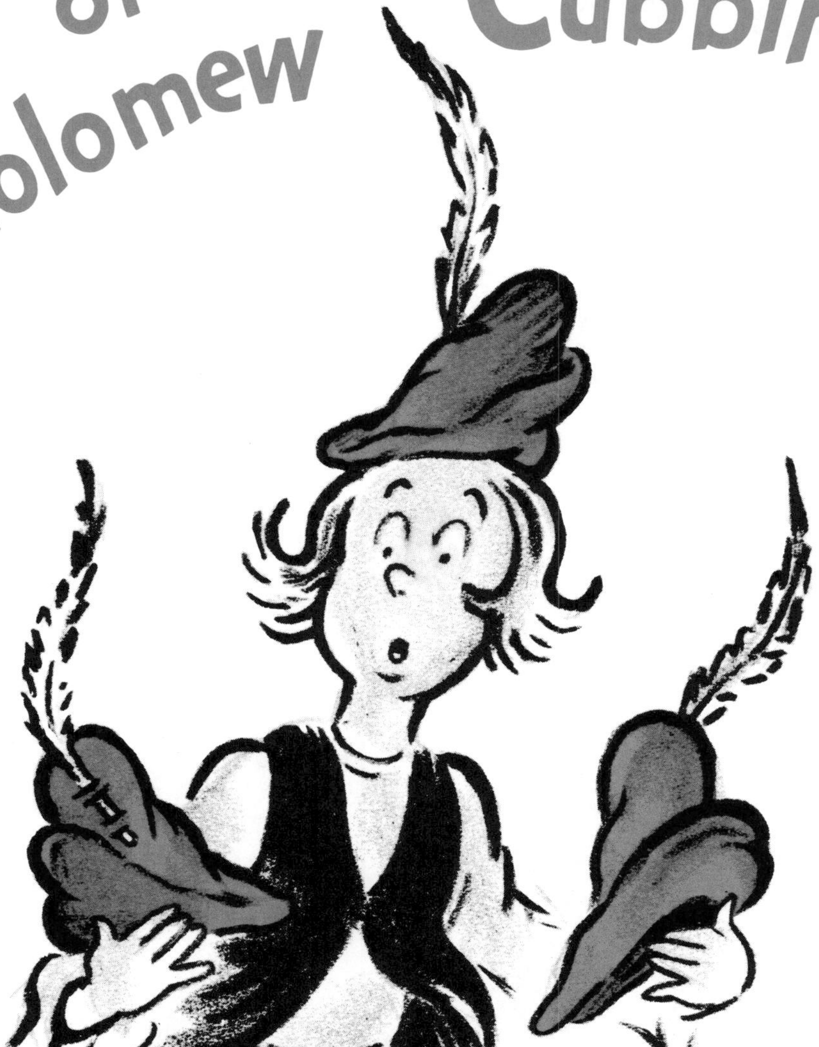

IN THE beginning, Bartholomew Cubbins didn't have five hundred hats. He had only one hat. It was an old one that had belonged to his father and his father's father before him. It was probably the oldest and the plainest hat in the whole Kingdom of Didd, where Bartholomew Cubbins lived. But Bartholomew liked it—especially because of the feather that always pointed straight up in the air.

The Kingdom of Didd was ruled by King Derwin. His palace stood high on the top of the mountain. From his balcony, he looked down over the houses of all his subjects—first, over the spires of the noblemen's castles, across the broad roofs of the rich men's mansions, then over the little houses of the townsfolk, to the huts of the farmers far off in the fields.

It was a mighty view and it made King Derwin feel mighty important.

Far off in the fields, on the edge of a cranberry bog, stood the hut of the Cubbins family. From the small door Bartholomew looked across the huts of the farmers to the houses of the townsfolk, then to the rich men's mansions and the noblemen's castles, up to the great towering palace of the King. It was exactly the same view that King Derwin saw from his balcony, but Bartholomew saw it backward.

It was a mighty view, but it made Bartholomew Cubbins feel mighty small.

Just after sunrise one Saturday morning Bartholomew started for town. He felt very happy. A pleasant breeze whistled through the feather in his hat. In his right hand he carried a basket of cranberries to sell at the market. He was anxious to sell them quickly and bring the money back home to his parents.

He walked faster and faster till he got to the gates of the town.

The sound of silver trumpets rang through the air. Hoof beats clattered on the cobbled streets.

"Clear the way! Clear the way! Make way for the King!"

All the people rushed for the sidewalks. They drove their carts right up over the curbstones. Bartholomew clutched his basket tighter.

Around the corner dashed fifty trumpeters on yellow-robed horses. Behind them on crimson-robed horses came the King's Own Guards.

"Hats off to the King!" shouted the Captain of the King's Own Guards.

On came the King's carriage — white and gold and purple. It rumbled like thunder through the narrow street.

It swept past Bartholomew. Then suddenly its mighty brakes shrieked. It lurched—and then it stopped. The whole procession stood still.

Bartholomew could hardly believe what he saw. Through the side window of the carriage, the King himself was staring back—straight back at him! Bartholomew began to tremble.

"Back up!" the King commanded the Royal Coachman.

The Royal Coachman shouted to the royal horses. The King's Own Guards shouted to their crimson-robed horses. The trumpeters shouted to their yellow-robed horses. Very slowly the whole procession backed down the street, until the King's carriage stopped right in front of Bartholomew.

The King leaned from his carriage window and fixed his eyes directly on Bartholomew Cubbins. "Well . . .? Well . . .?" he demanded.

Bartholomew shook with fright. "I ought to say something," he thought to himself. But he could think of nothing to say.

"Well?" demanded the King again. "Do you or do you *not* take off your hat before your King?"

"Yes, indeed, Sire," answered Bartholomew, feeling greatly relieved. "I *do* take off my hat before my King."

"Then take it off this very instant," commanded the King more loudly than before.

"But, Sire, my hat *is* off," answered Bartholomew.

"Such impudence!" shouted the King, shaking an angry finger. "How dare you stand there and tell me your hat is off!"

"I don't like to say you are wrong, Sire," said Bartholomew very politely, "but you see my hat *is* off." And he showed the King the hat in his hand.

"If that's your hat in your hand," demanded the King, "what's that on your head?"

"On my head?" gasped Bartholomew. There *did* seem to be something on his head. He reached up his hand and touched a hat!

The face of Bartholomew Cubbins turned very red. "It's a hat, Sire," he stammered, "but it *can't* be mine. Someone behind me must have put it on my head."

"I don't care *how* it got there," said the King. "You take it off." And the King sat back in his carriage.

Bartholomew quickly snatched off the hat. He stared at it in astonishment. It was exactly the same as his own hat—the same size, the same color. And it had exactly the same feather.

"By the Crown of my Fathers!" roared the King, again leaning out of the carriage window. "Did I or did I *not* command you to take off your hat?"

"You did, Sire. . . . I took it off . . . I took it off twice."

"Nonsense! There is still a hat upon your head."

"Another hat?" Again Bartholomew reached up his hand and touched a hat.

"Come, come, what is the meaning of all this?" demanded the King, his face purple with rage.

"I don't know, Sire," answered Bartholomew. "It never happened to me before."

The King was now shaking with such fury that the carriage rocked on its wheels and the Royal Coachman could hardly sit in his seat. "Arrest this impudent trickster," shouted the King to the Captain of the King's Own Guards. "We'll teach him to take off his hat."

The Royal Coachman cracked his long whip. The King's carriage swung forward up the street toward the palace.

But the Captain of the King's Own Guards leaned down from his big brass saddle and grabbed Bartholomew Cubbins by his shirt. Away flew Bartholomew's basket! The cranberries bounced over the cobblestones and rolled down into the gutter.

With a jangling of spurs and a clatter of horseshoes, the Captain and Bartholomew sped up the winding street toward the palace. Out of the narrow streets, on up the hill! Bartholomew clung to the Captain's broad back. On and on they galloped, past the bright gardens of the wealthy merchants. Higher and higher up the mountain, on past the walls of the noblemen's castles. . . .

Flupp! . . . the sharp wind whisked off Bartholomew's hat. *Flupp Flupp* . . . two more flew off. *Flupp Flupp Flupp* flew another . . . and another. ". . . 4 . . . 5 . . . 6 . . . 7 . . ." Bartholomew kept counting as the hats came faster and faster. Lords and ladies stared from the windows of their turrets, wondering what the strange stream of hats could mean.

Over the palace drawbridge they sped—through the great gates, and into the courtyard. The Captain pulled in his reins.

"His Majesty waits in the Throne Room," said a guard, saluting the Captain.

"The Throne Room!" The Captain dropped Bartholomew to the ground. "I'd certainly hate to be in your shoes," he said, shaking his head sadly.

For a moment Bartholomew was terribly frightened. "Still," he thought to himself, "the King can do nothing dreadful to punish me, because I really haven't done anything wrong. It would be cowardly to feel afraid."

Bartholomew threw back his shoulders and marched straight ahead into the palace. "Follow the black carpet," said the guard at the door. All through the long hallway Bartholomew could hear the muttering of voices behind heavy doors. "He won't take off his hat?" "No, he won't take off his hat."

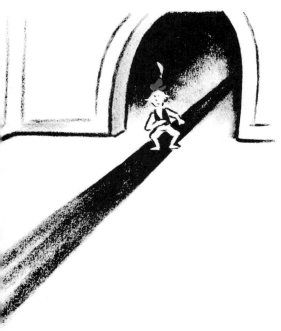

Bartholomew walked on till he stood
in the very middle of the Throne Room.
The King, in a long scarlet robe, was sitting on
his throne. Beside him stood Sir Alaric, Keeper of
the King's Records. He wore in his belt, instead of a
sword, a long silver ruler. Lords and noblemen of the
court stood solemn and silent.

The King looked down at Bartholomew severely. "Young man,
I'll give you one more chance. Will you take off your hat for your
King?"

"Your Majesty," said Bartholomew as politely as he possibly could,
"I will—but I'm afraid it won't do any good." And he took off his hat—
and it didn't do any good. Another hat sat on Bartholomew's head.
He took off hat after hat after hat after hat until he was standing in the
middle of a great pile of hats.

The lords and noblemen were so astonished they couldn't even
speak. Such a thing had never happened in the Throne Room before.

"Heavens!" said Sir Alaric, Keeper of the Records, blinking behind his triangular spectacles. "He's taken off 45!"

"And there were 3 more down in the town," said the King.

"And you must add on 87 more that blew off my head as we galloped up the hill," said Bartholomew, trying to be helpful.

"One hundred and thirty-five hats! Most unusual," said Sir Alaric, writing it down on a long scroll.

"Come, come," said the King impatiently. "Sir Alaric, what do you make of all this nonsense?"

"Very *serious* nonsense, Your Majesty," answered Sir Alaric. "I advise you to call in an expert on hats."

"Excellent," agreed the King. "Ho, Guard! Fetch in Sir Snipps, maker of hats for all the fine lords."

Into the Throne Room marched the smallest man, wearing the tallest hat that Bartholomew had ever seen. It was Sir Snipps. Instead of a sword, he wore at his side a large pair of scissors.

"Take a look at this boy's hat," commanded the King. Sir Snipps looked at Bartholomew Cubbins' hat and sniffed in disgust. Then he turned to the King and bowed stiffly. "Your Majesty, I, Sir Snipps, am the maker of hats for all the fine lords. I make hats of cloth of gold, fine silks and gems and ostrich plumes. You ask *me* what *I* think of *this* hat? Pooh! It is the most ordinary hat I ever set eyes on."

"In that case," said the King, "it should be very simple for you to take it off."

"Simple, indeed," mumbled Sir Snipps haughtily, and, standing on his tiptoes, he pushed his pudgy thumb at Bartholomew's hat and knocked it to the floor. Immediately another appeared on Bartholomew's head.

"Screebees!" screamed Sir Snipps, leaping in the air higher than he was tall. Then he turned and ran shrieking out of the Throne Room.

"Dear me!" said the King, looking very puzzled. "If Snipps can't do it, this *must* be more than an ordinary hat."

"One hundred and thirty-six," wrote Sir Alaric, wrinkling his brow. "Your Majesty, I advise that you call in your Wise Men."

"A fine idea!" said the King. "Ho, Guard! bring me Nadd. Nadd knows about everything in all my kingdom."

In came an old, old man. He looked at the hat on Bartholomew's head, and he looked at the pile of hats on the floor.

"Nadd, my Wise Man, can you take off his hat?" asked the King. Nadd shook his head solemnly—solemnly no.

"Then fetch me the Father of Nadd," commanded the King. "He knows about everything in all my kingdom and in all the world beyond."

In came an even older man. But when he looked at Bartholomew's hats, the Father of Nadd merely locked his fingers across his beard and said nothing.

"Then bring me the Father of the Father of Nadd!" ordered the King. "He knows about everything in all my kingdom, in all the world beyond, and in all other worlds that may happen to be."

Then came the oldest man of them all. But he just looked at Bartholomew and nibbled nervously at the end of his beard.

"Does this mean there is *no one* in my whole kingdom who can take off this boy's hat?" bellowed the King in a terrifying voice.

A small voice came up through the balcony window. "What's the matter, Uncle Derwin?" To Bartholomew, it sounded like the voice of a boy.

The King stepped out on the balcony and leaned over the marble railing. "There's a boy in here . . . just about your age," the King said. "He won't take off his hat."

Bartholomew tiptoed up behind the King and looked down. There stood a boy with a big lace collar—a very proud little boy with his nose in the air. It was the Grand Duke Wilfred, nephew of the King.

"You send him down here," said the Grand Duke Wilfred. *"I'll* fix him."

The King thought for a minute. He pushed back his crown and scratched his head. "Well . . . maybe you can. There's no harm trying."

"Take him to the Grand Duke Wilfred!" commanded the King. And two of the King's Own Guards led Bartholomew out of the Throne Room.

"Pooh!" said the Grand Duke Wilfred, looking at Bartholomew's hat and laughing meanly. "*That* hat won't come off? You stand over there." He pointed to a corner where the wall curved out. "I need a little target practise with my bow and arrow."

When Bartholomew saw that the Grand Duke Wilfred had only a child's bow he didn't feel frightened. He spoke up proudly, "*I* can shoot with my father's big bow."

"My bow's plenty big enough for shooting hats—especially hats like yours," answered Wilfred. And he let fly an arrow. zzZ! . . . it grazed Bartholomew's forehead and nipped off his hat. Away it blew, and over the parapet. But another hat appeared on his head. zzZ! . . . zzZ! . . . zzZ! . . . the arrows flew . . . till the Grand Duke's whole bagful of arrows was gone. And still a hat sat upon Bartholomew's head.

"It's not fair," cried the Grand Duke. "It's not fair!" He threw down his bow and stamped upon it.

"One hundred and fifty-four hats!" gulped Sir Alaric.

"These hats are driving me mad!" The King's voice rang out through all the palace. "Why waste time with a *child's* bow and arrow. Fetch me the mightiest bow and arrow in all my realm—fetch the Yeoman of the Bowmen!"

"Yeoman of the Bowmen," echoed all the lords and noblemen of the court.

A gigantic man strode out across the terrace. His bow was as big as the branch of a tree. The arrow was twice as long as Bartholomew, and thicker than his wrist.

"Yeoman of the Bowmen," said the King, "shoot off this boy's hat . . . and make it *stay* off!"

Bartholomew was trembling so hard that he could scarcely stand straight. The Yeoman bent back his mighty bow.

G—r—r—zibb! . . . Like a mad giant hornet the arrow tore through the air toward Bartholomew Cubbins.

G—r—r—zapp! . . . The sharp arrow head bit through his hat and carried it off—on and on for a full half mile.

G—r—r—zopp! . . . It plunked to a stop in the heart of an oak tree. Yet there on Bartholomew's head sat another hat.

The face of the Yeoman of the Bowmen went white as the palace walls. "It's black magic!" he shrieked.

"Black magic, that's *just* what it is," sighed the King with relief. "I should have thought of that before. That makes things simple. Back to the Throne Room! Call my magicians!"

In the whole Throne Room there wasn't a sound as loud as a breath. But from the spiral stairs that led down from the southwest tower came the shuffling of slow, padded feet. The magicians were coming! Low and slow, they were chanting words that were strange . . .

> *"Dig a hole five furlongs deep,*
> *Down to where the night snakes creep,*
> *Mix and mold the mystic mud,*
> *Malber, Balber, Tidder, Tudd."*

In came seven black-gowned magicians, and beside each one stalked a lean black cat. They circled around Bartholomew Cubbins muttering deep and mysterious sounds.

"Stop this useless muttering," ordered the King. "I want a chant that will charm away this boy's hat."

The magicians huddled over Bartholomew and chanted.

> *"Winkibus*
> *Tinkibus*
> *Fotichee*
> *Klay,*
> *Hat on this demon's head,*
> *Fly far away!*
> *Howl, men, howl away,*
> *Howl away, howl away,*
> *Yowl, cats, yowl away,*
> *Yowl away, yowl away!*
> *Hat on this demon's head,*
> *Seep away, creep away, leap away, gleap away,*
> > *Never come back!"*

"A mighty good chant," said the King, looking very pleased. "Are you sure it will work?"

All the magicians nodded together.

"But," said the King, looking puzzled, "there still *seems* to be a hat upon his head. How long will it take for the charm to work?"

"Be calm, oh, Sire, and have no fears," chanted the magicians.

"Our charm will work in ten short years."

"Ten years!" gasped the King. "Away, fools!" he shouted. "Out of my sight! I can't wait *ten years* to get rid of his hat. Oh, dear, what *can* I do . . . what CAN I do?"

"If I were King," whispered the Grand Duke Wilfred, "I'd chop off his head."

"A dreadful thought," said the King, biting his lip. "But I'm afraid I'll have to."

"Young man," he said to Bartholomew Cubbins, and he pointed to a small door at the end of the room, "march down those steps to the dungeon and tell the executioner to chop off your head."

Bartholomew's heart sank into his boots, but he did as the King commanded. "I *must* take off my hat," he said to himself as he started down the long black stairway. "This is my last chance." One

hat after another he tore from his head "...156...157...158..." It grew colder and damper. "...217...218...219..." Down... down...down. "...231...232...233..." It seemed to Bartholomew he must be in the very heart of the mountain.

"Who's there?" said a voice from the blackness.

Bartholomew turned a corner and stepped into the dungeon.

The executioner was whistling and swinging his axe idly, because at the moment he had nothing to do. In spite of his business, he really seemed to be a very pleasant man.

"The King says you must chop off my head," said Bartholomew.

"Oh, I'd hate to," said the executioner, looking at him with a friendly smile. "You seem like such a nice boy."

"Well . . . the King says you have to," said Bartholomew, "so please get it over with."

"All right," sighed the executioner, "but first you've got to take off your hat."

"Why?" asked Bartholomew.

"I don't know," said the executioner, "but it's one of the rules. I can't execute anyone with his hat on."

"All right," said Bartholomew, "you take it off for me."

The executioner leaned across the chopping block and flipped off Bartholomew's hat.

"What's this?" he gasped, blinking through the holes in his mask, as another hat sat on Bartholomew's head. He flipped this one off . . . then another and another.

"Fiddlesticks!" grunted the executioner, throwing his axe on the floor. "I can't execute you at all." And he shook hands with Bartholomew and sent him back upstairs to the King.

The King had been taking a nap on the throne. "What are you doing back here?" he said to Bartholomew, angry at being awakened.

"I'm sorry, Your Majesty," explained Bartholomew. "My head can't come off with my hat on. . . . It's against the rules."

"So it can't," said the King, leaning back wearily. "Now how many hats does that make altogether?"

"The executioner knocked off 13 . . . and I left 178 more on the dungeon steps," answered Bartholomew.

"Three hundred and forty-six hats," mumbled Sir Alaric from behind his scroll.

"Uncle Derwin," yawned the Grand Duke Wilfred, "I suppose I'll have to do away with him. Send him up to the highest turret and I, in person, will push him off."

"Wilfred! I'm surprised at you," said the King. "But I guess it's a good idea."

So the King and the Grand Duke led Bartholomew Cubbins toward the highest turret.

Up and up and up the turret stairs he climbed behind them.

"This is my *last*—my *very last* chance," thought Bartholomew. He snatched off his hat. "Three hundred and forty-seven!" He snatched off another. He pulled and he tore and he flung them behind him. ". . . 398 . . 399 . . ." His arms ached from pulling off hats. But still the hats came. Bartholomew climbed on.

". . . 448 . . . 449 . . . 450 . . ." counted Sir Alaric, puffing up the stairs behind him.

Suddenly Sir Alaric stopped. He looked. He took off his triangular spectacles and wiped them on his sleeve. And then he looked again. *The hats began to change!* Hat 451 had, not one, but *two* feathers! Hat 452 had three . . . and 453 also had three *and a little red jewel!* Each new hat was fancier than the hat just before.

"Your Majesty! Your Majesty!" cried out Sir Alaric.

But the King and the Grand Duke were 'way up where they couldn't hear. They had already reached the top of the highest turret. Bartholomew was following just behind.

"Step right out here and get out on that wall," snapped the Grand Duke Wilfred. "I can't wait to push you off."

But when Bartholomew stepped up on the wall they gasped in amazement. He was wearing the most beautiful hat that had ever been seen in the Kingdom of Didd. It had a ruby larger than any the King himself had ever owned. It had ostrich plumes, and cockatoo plumes, and mockingbird plumes, and paradise plumes. Beside *such* a hat even the King's Crown seemed like nothing.

The Grand Duke Wilfred took a quick step forward. Bartholomew thought his end had come at last.

"Wait!" shouted the King. He could not take his eyes off the magnificent hat.

"I *won't* wait," the Grand Duke talked back to the King. "I'm going to push him off now! That new big hat makes me madder than ever." And he flung out his arms to push Bartholomew off.

But the King was quicker than Wilfred. He grabbed him by the back of his fine lace collar. "This is to teach you," His Majesty said sternly, "that Grand Dukes *never* talk back to their King." And he turned the Grand Duke Wilfred over his knee and spanked him soundly, right on the seat of his royal silk pants.

"And now," smiled the King, lifting Bartholomew down from the wall, "it would be nice if you'd sell me that wonderful hat!"

"... 498 ... 499 ..." broke in the tired voice of Sir Alaric, who had just arrived at the top of the steps, "and *that* ..." he pointed to the hat on Bartholomew's head, "makes exactly 500!"

"Five Hundred!" exclaimed the King. "Will you sell it for 500 pieces of gold?"

"Anything you say, Sire," answered Bartholomew. "You see ... I've never sold one before."

The King's hands trembled with joy as he reached for the hat.

Slowly, slowly, Bartholomew felt the weight of the great hat lifting from his head. He held his breath. . . . Then suddenly he felt the cool evening breezes blow through his hair. His face broke into a happy smile. The head of Bartholomew Cubbins was bare!

"Look, Your Majesty! *Look!*" he shouted to the King.

"No! *You* look at *me*," answered the King. And he put the great hat on right over his crown.

Arm in arm, the King and Bartholomew went down to the counting room to count out the gold. Then the King sent Bartholomew home to his parents . . . no basket on his arm, no hat on his head, but with five hundred pieces of gold in a bag.

And the King commanded that the hat he had bought, and all the other hats, too, be kept forever in a great crystal case by the side of his throne.

But neither Bartholomew Cubbins, nor King Derwin himself, nor anyone else in the Kingdom of Didd could ever explain how the strange thing had happened. They only could say it just "happened to happen" and was not very likely to happen again.

Horton Hatches the Egg

Sighed Mayzie, a lazy bird hatching an egg:
"I'm tired and I'm bored
And I've kinks in my leg
From sitting, just sitting here day after day.
It's *work!* How I hate it!
I'd *much* rather play!
I'd take a vacation, fly off for a rest
If I could find *someone* to stay on my nest!

If I could find someone, I'd fly away—free. . . ."

Then Horton, the Elephant, passed by her tree.

"Hello!" called the lazy bird, smiling her best,
"You've nothing to do and I *do* need a rest.
Would YOU like to sit on the egg in my nest?"

The elephant laughed.
"Why, of all silly things!
I haven't feathers and *I* haven't wings.
ME on your egg? Why, that doesn't make sense. . . .
Your egg is so small, ma'am, and I'm so immense!"

"Tut, tut," answered Mayzie. "I know you're not small
But I'm *sure* you can do it. No trouble at all.
Just sit on it softly. You're gentle and kind.
Come, be a good fellow. I know you won't mind."

"I can't," said the elephant.
"PL-E-E-ASE!" begged the bird.
"I won't be gone long, sir. I give you my word.
I'll hurry right back. Why, I'll never be missed. . . ."

"Very well," said the elephant, "since you insist. . . .

You want a vacation. Go fly off and take it.
I'll sit on your egg and I'll try not to break it.
I'll stay and be faithful. I mean what I say."

"Toodle-oo!" sang out Mayzie and fluttered away.

"H-m-m-m . . . the first thing to do," murmured Horton,
"Let's see. . . .
The first thing to do is to prop up this tree
And make it much stronger. That *has* to be done
Before I get on it. I must weigh a ton."

Then carefully,
Tenderly,
Gently he crept
Up the trunk to the nest where the little egg slept.

Then Horton the elephant smiled. "Now that's that. . . ."

And he sat
          and he sat
                    and he sat
                              and he sat. . . .

And he sat all that day
And he kept the egg warm. . . .
And he sat all that night
Through a *terrible* storm.
It poured and it lightninged!
It thundered! It rumbled!
"This isn't much fun,"
The poor elephant grumbled.
"I wish she'd come back
'Cause I'm cold and I'm wet.
I hope that that Mayzie bird doesn't forget."

But Mayzie, by this time, was far beyond reach,
Enjoying the sunshine way off in Palm Beach,
And having *such* fun, such a wonderful rest,

Decided she'd NEVER go back to her nest!

So Horton kept sitting there, day after day.
And soon it was Autumn. The leaves blew away.
And then came the Winter . . . the snow and the sleet!
And icicles hung
From his trunk and his feet.

But Horton kept sitting, and said with a sneeze,
"I'll *stay* on this egg and I *won't* let it freeze.
I meant what I said
And I said what I meant. . . .
An elephant's faithful
One hundred per cent!"

So poor Horton sat there
The whole winter through. . . .
And then came the springtime
With troubles anew!
His friends gathered round
And they shouted with glee.

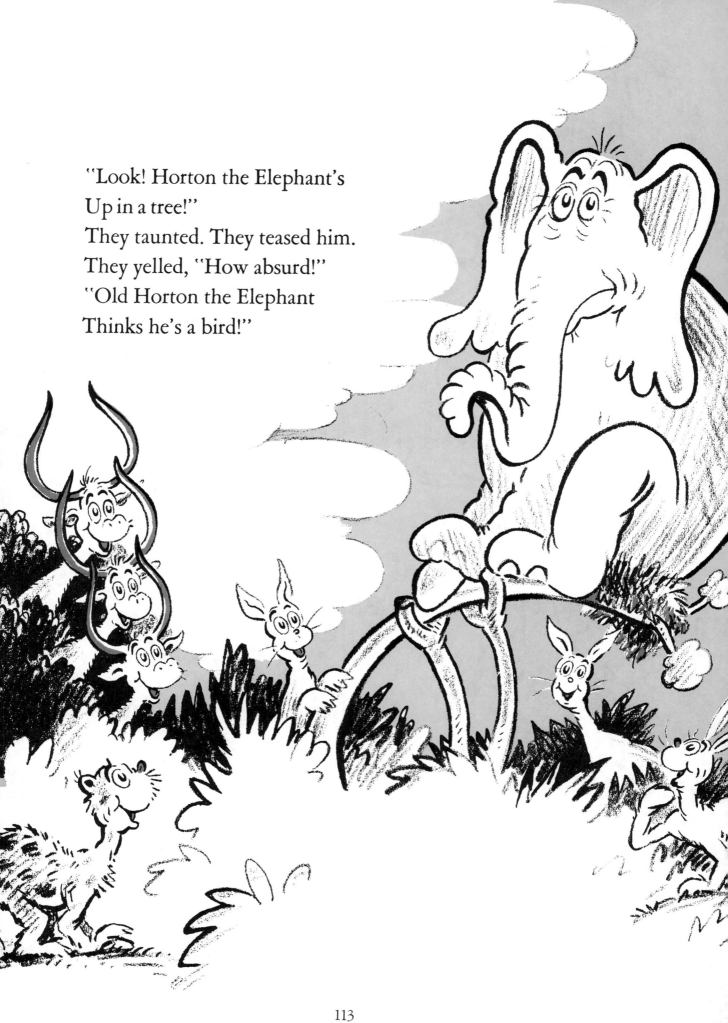

"Look! Horton the Elephant's
Up in a tree!"
They taunted. They teased him.
They yelled, "How absurd!"
"Old Horton the Elephant
Thinks he's a bird!"

They laughed and they laughed. Then they all ran away.
And Horton was lonely. He wanted to play.
But he sat on the egg and continued to say:
"I meant what I said
And I said what I meant. . . .
An elephant's faithful
One hundred per cent!

"No matter WHAT happens,
This egg must be tended!"

But poor Horton's troubles
Were far, far from ended.
For, while Horton sat there
So faithful, so kind,
Three hunters came sneaking
Up softly behind!

He heard the men's footsteps!
He turned with a start!
Three rifles were aiming
Right straight at his heart!

Did he run?
He did not!
HORTON STAYED ON THAT NEST!
He held his head high
And he threw out his chest
And he looked at the hunters
As much as to say:
"Shoot if you must
But I *won't* run away!
I meant what I said
And I said what I meant. . . .
An elephant's faithful
One hundred per cent!"

But the men *didn't* shoot!
Much to Horton's surprise,
They dropped their three guns
And they stared with wide eyes!
"Look!" they all shouted,
"Can such a thing be?
An elephant sitting on top of a tree . . ."

"It's strange! It's amazing! It's wonderful! New!
Don't shoot him. We'll CATCH him. That's *just* what we'll do!
Let's take him alive. Why, he's terribly funny!
We'll sell him back home to a circus, for money!"

And the first thing he knew, they had built a big wagon
With ropes on the front for the pullers to drag on.
They dug up his tree and they put it inside,
With Horton so sad that he practically cried.
"We're off!" the men shouted. And off they all went
With Horton unhappy, one hundred per cent.

Up out of the jungle! Up into the sky!
Up over the mountains ten thousand feet high!
Then down, down the mountains
And down to the sea
Went the cart with the elephant,
Egg, nest and tree . . .

Then out of the wagon
And onto a ship!
Out over the ocean . . .
And oooh, what a trip!
Rolling and tossing and splashed with the spray!
And Horton said, day after day after day,
"I meant what I said
And I said what I meant . . .
But oh, am I seasick!
One hundred per cent!"

After bobbing around for two weeks like a cork,
They landed at last in the town of New York.
"All ashore!" the men shouted,
And down with a lurch
Went Horton the Elephant
Still on his perch,
Tied onto a board that could just scarcely hold him. . . .

BUMP!
Horton landed!
And then the men sold him!

Sold to a circus! Then week after week
They showed him to people at ten cents a peek.
They took him to Boston, to Kalamazoo,
Chicago, Weehawken and Washington, too;
To Dayton, Ohio; St. Paul, Minnesota;
To Wichita, Kansas; to Drake, North Dakota.
And everywhere thousands of folks flocked to see
And laugh at the elephant up in a tree.
Poor Horton grew sadder the farther he went,
But he said as he sat in the hot noisy tent:
"I meant what I said, and I said what I meant . . .
An elephant's faithful—one hundred per cent!"

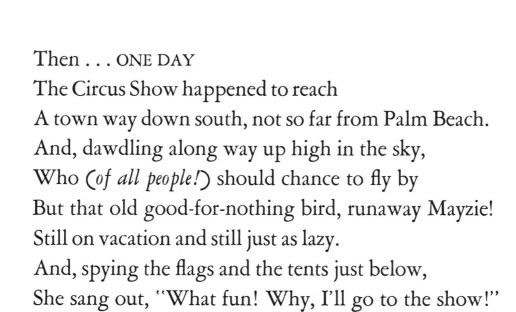

Then . . . ONE DAY
The Circus Show happened to reach
A town way down south, not so far from Palm Beach.
And, dawdling along way up high in the sky,
Who (*of all people!*) should chance to fly by
But that old good-for-nothing bird, runaway Mayzie!
Still on vacation and still just as lazy.
And, spying the flags and the tents just below,
She sang out, "What fun! Why, I'll go to the show!"

And she swooped from the clouds
Through an open tent door . . .
"Good gracious!" gasped Mayzie,
"I've seen YOU *before!"*

Poor Horton looked up with his face white as chalk!
He started to speak, but before he could talk . . .

There rang out the noisiest ear-splitting squeaks
From the egg that he'd sat on for fifty-one weeks!
A thumping! A bumping! A wild alive scratching!
"My egg!" shouted Horton. "My EGG! WHY, IT'S HATCHING!"

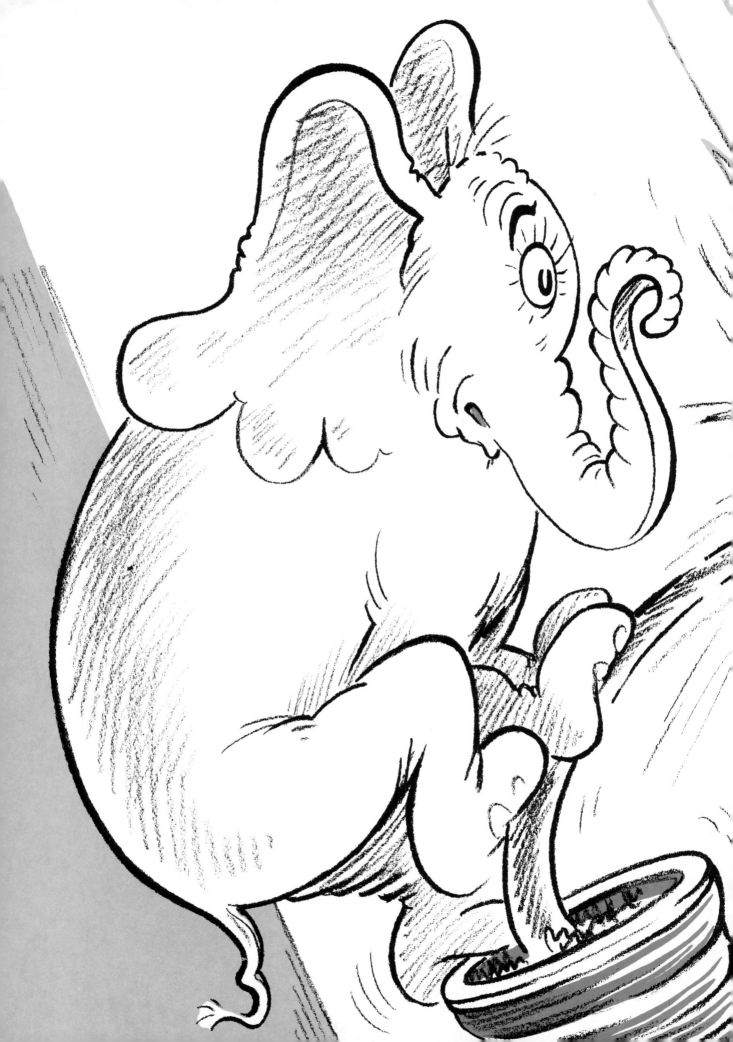

"But it's MINE!" screamed the bird, when she heard the egg crack.
(The work was all done. Now she wanted it back.)
"It's MY egg!" she sputtered. "You stole it from me!
Get off of my nest and get out of my tree!"

Poor Horton backed down
With a sad, heavy heart. . . .

But at that very instant, the egg burst apart!
And out of the pieces of red and white shell,
From the egg that he'd sat on so long and so well,
Horton the Elephant saw something whizz!
IT HAD EARS

　　　AND A TAIL

　　　　　　AND A TRUNK JUST LIKE HIS!

And the people came shouting, *"What's all this about . . .?"*
They looked! And they stared with their eyes popping out!
Then they cheered and they *cheered* and they CHEERED more and more.
They'd never seen anything like it before!
"My goodness! *My gracious!"* they shouted. "MY WORD!
It's something brand new!
IT'S AN ELEPHANT-BIRD!!

And it should be, it *should* be, it SHOULD be like that!

Because Horton was faithful! He sat and he sat!

He meant what he said

And he said what he meant. . . ."

. . . And they sent him home
Happy,
One hundred per cent!

YERTLE the TURTLE

and
Other Stories

YERTLE the TURTLE

On the far-away Island of Sala-ma-Sond,
Yertle the Turtle was king of the pond.
A nice little pond. It was clean. It was neat.
The water was warm. There was plenty to eat.
The turtles had everything turtles might need.
And they were all happy. Quite happy indeed.

They *were* . . . until Yertle, the king of them all,
Decided the kingdom he ruled was too small.
"I'm ruler," said Yertle, "of all that I see.
But I don't see *enough*. That's the trouble with me.
With this stone for a throne, I look down on my pond
But I cannot look down on the places beyond.
This throne that I sit on is too, too low down.
It ought to be *higher*!" he said with a frown.
"If I could sit high, how much greater I'd be!
What a king! I'd be ruler of all I could see!"

So Yertle, the Turtle King, lifted his hand
And Yertle, the Turtle King, gave a command.
He ordered nine turtles to swim to his stone
And, using these turtles, he built a *new* throne.
He made each turtle stand on another one's back
And he piled them all up in a nine-turtle stack.
And then Yertle climbed up. He sat down on the pile.
What a wonderful view! He could see 'most a mile!

"All mine!" Yertle cried. "Oh, the things I now rule!
I'm king of a cow! And I'm king of a mule!
I'm king of a house! And, what's more, beyond that,
I'm king of a blueberry bush and a cat!
I'm Yertle the Turtle! Oh, marvelous me!
For I am the ruler of all that I see!"

And all through that morning, he sat there up high
Saying over and over, "A great king am I!"
Until 'long about noon. Then he heard a faint sigh.
"What's *that*?" snapped the king
And he looked down the stack.
And he saw, at the bottom, a turtle named Mack.
Just a part of his throne. And this plain little turtle
Looked up and he said, "Beg your pardon, King Yertle.
"I've pains in my back and my shoulders and knees.
How long must we stand here, Your Majesty, please?"

"SILENCE!" the King of the Turtles barked back.
"I'm king, and you're only a turtle named Mack."

"You stay in your place while I sit here and rule.
I'm king of a cow! And I'm king of a mule!
I'm king of a house! And a bush! And a cat!
But that isn't all. I'll do better than *that*!
My throne shall be *higher*!" his royal voice thundered,
"So pile up more turtles! I want 'bout two hundred!"

"Turtles! More turtles!" he bellowed and brayed.
And the turtles 'way down in the pond were afraid.
They trembled. They shook. But they came. They obeyed.
From all over the pond, they came swimming by dozens.
Whole families of turtles, with uncles and cousins.
And all of them stepped on the head of poor Mack.
One after another, they climbed up the stack.

THEN Yertle the Turtle was perched up so high,
He could see forty miles from his throne in the sky!
"Hooray!" shouted Yertle. "I'm king of the trees!
I'm king of the birds! And I'm king of the bees!
I'm king of the butterflies! King of the air!
Ah, me! What a throne! What a wonderful chair!
I'm Yertle the Turtle! Oh, marvelous me!
For I am the ruler of all that I see!"

Then again, from below, in the great heavy stack,
Came a groan from that plain little turtle named Mack.
"Your Majesty, please...I don't like to complain,
But down here below, we are feeling great pain.
I know, up on top you are seeing great sights,
But down at the bottom we, too, should have rights.
We turtles can't stand it. Our shells will all crack!
Besides, we need food. We are starving!" groaned Mack.

"You hush up your mouth!" howled the mighty King Yertle.
"You've no right to talk to the world's highest turtle.
I rule from the clouds! Over land! Over sea!
There's nothing, no, NOTHING, that's higher than me!"

But, while he was shouting, he saw with surprise
That the moon of the evening was starting to rise
Up over his head in the darkening skies.
"What's THAT?" snorted Yertle. "Say, what IS that thing
That dares to be higher than Yertle the King?
I shall not allow it! I'll go higher still!
I'll build my throne higher! I can and I will!
I'll call some more turtles. I'll stack 'em to heaven!
I need 'bout five thousand, six hundred and seven!"

But, as Yertle, the Turtle King, lifted his hand
And started to order and give the command,
That plain little turtle below in the stack,
That plain little turtle whose name was just Mack,
Decided he'd taken enough. And he had.
And that plain little lad got a little bit mad
And that plain little Mack did a plain little thing.
He burped!
And his burp shook the throne of the king!

And Yertle the Turtle, the king of the trees,
The king of the air and the birds and the bees,
The king of a house and a cow and a mule...
Well, *that* was the end of the Turtle King's rule!
For Yertle, the King of all Sala-ma-Sond,
Fell off his high throne and fell *Plunk*! in the pond!

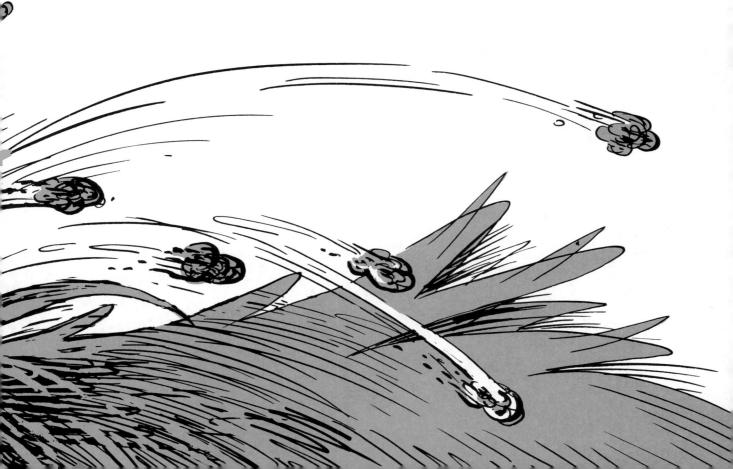

And today the great Yertle, that Marvelous he,
Is King of the Mud. That is all he can see.
And the turtles, of course...all the turtles are free
As turtles and, maybe, all creatures should be.

GERTRUDE McFUZZ

There once was a girl-bird named Gertrude McFuzz
And she had the smallest plain tail ever was.
One droopy-droop feather. That's all that she had.
And, oh! That one feather made Gertrude so sad.

For there was another young bird that she knew,
A fancy young birdie named Lolla-Lee-Lou,
And instead of *one* feather behind, she had *two*!
Poor Gertrude! Whenever she happened to spy
Miss Lolla-Lee-Lou flying by in the sky,
She got very jealous. She frowned. And she pouted.
Then, one day she got awfully mad and she shouted:
"This just isn't fair! I have *one*! She has *two*!
I MUST have a tail just like Lolla-Lee-Lou!"

So she flew to her uncle, a doctor named Dake
Whose office was high in a tree by the lake
And she cried, "Uncle Doctor! Oh, please do you know
Of some kind of a pill that will make my tail grow?"
"Tut tut!" said the doctor. "Such talk! How absurd!
Your tail is just right for your kind of a bird."

Then Gertrude had tantrums. She raised such a din
That finally her uncle, the doctor, gave in
And he told her just where she could find such a pill
On a pill-berry vine on the top of the hill.
"Oh, thank you!" chirped Gertrude McFuzz, and she flew
Right straight to the hill where the pill-berry grew.

Yes! There was the vine! And as soon as she saw it
She plucked off a berry. She started to gnaw it.
It tasted just awful. Almost made her sick.
But she wanted that tail, so she swallowed it quick.
Then she felt something happen! She felt a small twitch
As if she'd been tapped, down behind, by a switch.
And Gertrude looked 'round. And she cheered! It was true!
Two feathers! Exactly like Lolla-Lee-Lou!

Then she got an idea! "Now I know what I'll do...
I'll grow a tail *better* than Lolla-Lee-Lou!"

"These pills that grow feathers are working just fine!"
So she nibbled *another* one off of the vine!

She felt a *new* twitch. And then Gertrude yelled, "WHEE!
Miss Lolla has only just *two*! I have *three*!
When Lolla-Lee-Lou sees this beautiful stuff,
She'll fall right down flat on her face, sure enough!
I'll show HER who's pretty! I certainly will!
Why, I'll make my tail even prettier still!"

She snatched at those berries that grew on that vine.
She gobbled down four, five, six, seven, eight, nine!
And she didn't stop eating, young Gertrude McFuzz,
Till she'd eaten three dozen! That's all that there was.

Then the feathers popped out! With a *zang*! With a *zing*!
They blossomed like flowers that bloom in the spring.
All fit for a queen! What a sight to behold!
They sparkled like diamonds and gumdrops and gold!
Like silk! Like spaghetti! Like satin! Like lace!
They burst out like rockets all over the place!
They waved in the air and they swished in the breeze!
And some were as long as the branches of trees.
And *still* they kept growing! They popped and they popped
Until, 'long about sundown when, finally, they stopped.

"And NOW," giggled Gertrude, "The next thing to do
Is to fly right straight home and show Lolla-Lee-Lou!
And when Lolla sees *these*, why her face will get red
And she'll let out a scream and she'll fall right down dead!"

Then she spread out her wings to take off from the ground,
But, with all of those feathers, she weighed ninety pound!
She yanked and she pulled and she let out a squawk,
But that bird couldn't fly! Couldn't run! Couldn't walk!

And all through that night, she was stuck on that hill,
And Gertrude McFuzz might be stuck up there still
If her good Uncle Dake hadn't heard the girl yelp.
He rushed to her rescue and brought along help.

To lift Gertrude up almost broke all their beaks
And to fly her back home, it took almost two weeks.
And *then* it took almost another week more
To pull out those feathers. My! Gertrude was sore!

And, finally, when all of the pulling was done,
Gertrude, behind her, again had just one . . .
That one little feather she had as a starter.
But now that's enough, because now she is smarter.

The BIG BRAG

The rabbit felt mighty important that day
On top of the hill in the sun where he lay.
He felt SO important up there on that hill
That he started in bragging, as animals will
And he boasted out loud, as he threw out his chest,
"Of all of the beasts in the world, I'm the best!
On land, and on sea ... even up in the sky
No animal lives who is better than I!"

"What's *that?*" growled a voice that was terribly gruff.
"Now why do you say such ridiculous stuff?"
The rabbit looked down and he saw a big bear.
"*I'm* best of the beasts," said the bear. "And so there!"

"You're not!" snapped the rabbit. "I'm better than you!"
"Pooh!" the bear snorted. "Again I say Pooh!
You talk mighty big, Mr. Rabbit. That's true.
But how can you prove it? **Just what can you DO?"**

"Hmmmm..." thought the rabbit,
"Now what CAN I do...?"
He thought and he thought. Then he finally said,
"Mr. Bear, do you see these two ears on my head?
My ears are so keen and so sharp and so fine
No ears in the world can hear further than mine!"

"Humpf!" the bear grunted. He looked at each ear.
"You *say* they are good," said the bear with a sneer,
"But how do *I* know just how far they can hear?"

"I'll prove," said the rabbit, "my ears are the best.
You sit there and watch me. I'll prove it by test."
Then he stiffened his ears till they both stood up high
And pointed straight up at the blue of the sky.
He stretched his ears open as wide as he could.
"*Shhh!* I am listening!" he said as he stood.
He listened so hard that he started to sweat
And the fur on his ears and his forehead got wet.

For seven long minutes he stood. Then he stirred
And he said to the bear, "Do you know what I heard?
Do you see that far mountain . . . ? It's ninety miles off.
There's a fly on that mountain. I just heard him cough!
Now the cough of a fly, sir, is quite hard to hear
When he's ninety miles off. But I heard it quite clear.
So you see," bragged the rabbit, "it's perfectly true
That my ears are the best, so I'm better than you!"

The bear, for a moment, just sulked as he sat
For he knew that *his* ears couldn't hear things like *that*.
"This rabbit," he thought, "made a fool out of me.
Now *I've* got to prove that I'm better than he."
So he said to the rabbit, "You hear pretty well.
You can hear ninety miles. *But how far can you smell?*
I'm the greatest of smellers," he bragged. "See my nose?
This nose on my face is the finest that grows.
My nose can smell *any*thing, both far and near.
With my nose I can smell twice as far as you hear!"

"You can't!" snapped the rabbit.

"I can!" growled the bear

And he stuck his big nose 'way up high in the air.

He wiggled that nose and he sniffed and he snuffed.

He waggled that nose and he whiffed and he whuffed.

For more than ten minutes he snaff and he snuff.

Then he said to the rabbit, "I've smelled far enough."

"All right," said the rabbit. "Come on now and tell
Exactly how far is the smell that you smell?"

"Oh, I'm smelling a *very* far smell," said the bear.
"Away past that fly on that mountain out there.
I'm smelling past many great mountains beyond
Six hundred miles more to the edge of a pond."

"And 'way, 'way out there, by the pond you can't see,
Is a very small farm. On the farm is a tree.
On the tree is a branch. On the branch is a nest,
A very small nest where two tiny eggs rest.
Two hummingbird eggs! Only half an inch long!
But my nose," said the bear, "is so wonderfully strong,
My nose is so good that I smelled without fail
That the egg on the left is a little bit stale!
And *that* is a thing that no rabbit can do.
So you see," the bear boasted, "I'm better than you!
My smeller's so keen that it just can't be beat..."

"What's that?" called a voice
From 'way down by his feet.
The bear and the rabbit looked down at the sound,
And they saw an old worm crawling out of the ground.

"Now, boys," said the worm, "you've been bragging a lot.
You both think you're great. But *I* think you are not.
You're not half as good as a fellow like me.
You hear and you smell. *But how far can you SEE?*
Now, *I'm* here to prove to you big boasting guys
That your nose and your ears aren't as good as my eyes!"

And the little old worm cocked his head to one side
And he opened his eyes and he opened them wide.
And they looked far away with a strange sort of stare.
As if they were burning two holes in the air.
The eyes of that worm almost popped from his head.
He stared half an hour till his eyelids got red.
"That's enough!" growled the bear.
"Tell the rabbit and me
How far did you look and just what did you see?"

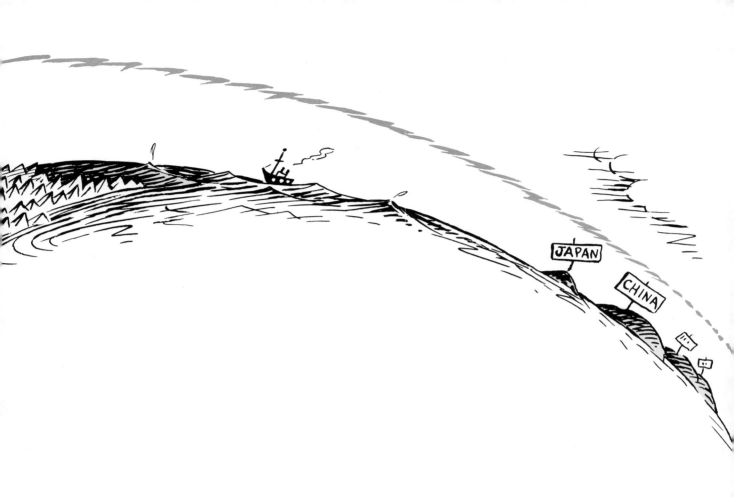

"Well, boys," the worm answered, "that look that I took
Was a look that looked farther than *you'll* ever look!
I looked 'cross the ocean, 'way out to Japan.
For I can see farther than anyone can.
There's no one on earth who has eyesight that's finer.
I looked past Japan. Then I looked across China.
I looked across Egypt; then took a quick glance
Across the two countries of Holland and France.
Then I looked across England and, also, Brazil.
But I didn't stop there. I looked much farther still.

"And I kept right on looking and looking until
I'd looked 'round the world and right back to this hill!
And I saw on this hill, since my eyesight's so keen,
The two biggest fools that have ever been seen!
And the fools that I saw were none other than you,
Who seem to have nothing else better to do
Than sit here and argue who's better than who!"

Then the little old worm gave his head a small jerk
And he dived in his hole and went back to his work.

Every *Who*
Down in *Who*-ville
Liked Christmas a lot...

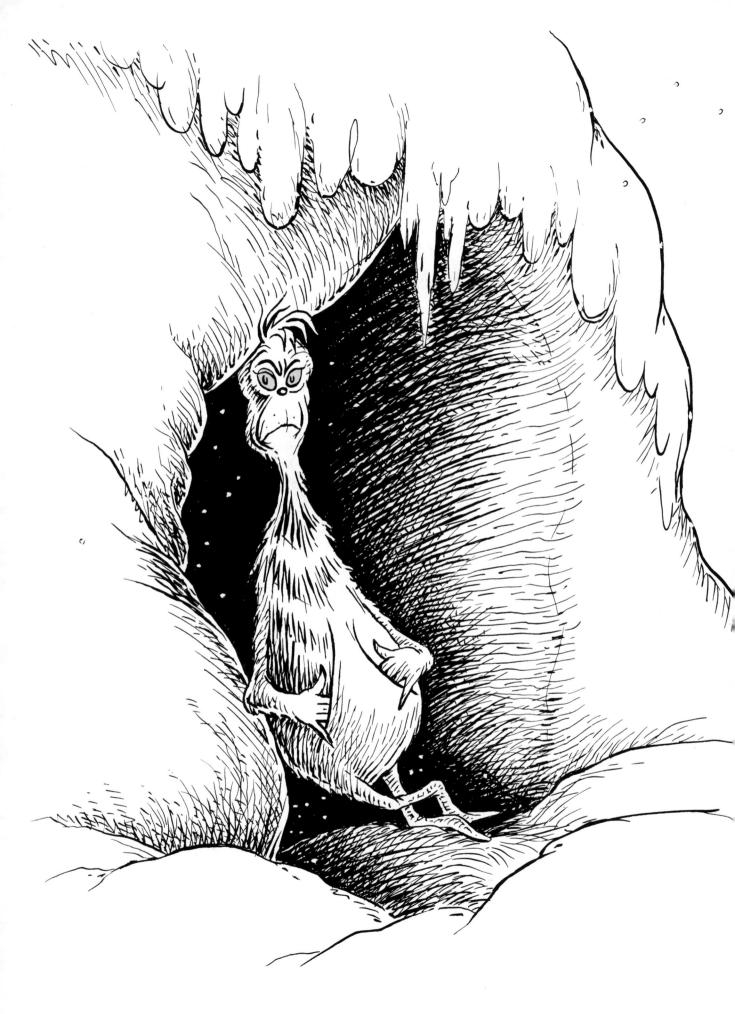

But the Grinch,
Who lived just north of *Who*-ville,
Did NOT!

The Grinch *hated* Christmas! The whole Christmas season!
Now, please don't ask why. No one quite knows the reason.
It *could* be his head wasn't screwed on just right.
It *could* be, perhaps, that his shoes were too tight.
But I think that the most likely reason of all
May have been that his heart was two sizes too small.

But,
Whatever the reason,
His heart or his shoes,
He stood there on Christmas Eve, hating the *Whos,*
Staring down from his cave with a sour, Grinchy frown
At the warm lighted windows below in their town.
For he knew every *Who* down in *Who*-ville beneath
Was busy now, hanging a mistletoe wreath.

"And they're hanging their stockings!" he snarled with a sneer.
"Tomorrow is Christmas! It's practically here!"
Then he growled, with his Grinch fingers nervously drumming,
"I MUST find some way to stop Christmas from coming!"

For,
Tomorrow, he knew . . .

MERRY MERRY

...All the *Who* girls and boys
Would wake bright and early. They'd rush for their toys!
And *then!* Oh, the noise! Oh, the Noise! Noise! Noise! Noise!
That's *one* thing he hated! The NOISE! NOISE! NOISE! NOISE!

Then the *Whos,* young and old, would sit down to a feast.
And they'd feast! *And they'd feast!*
And they'd FEAST!

FEAST!

FEAST!

FEAST!

They would feast on *Who*-pudding, and rare *Who*-roast-beast
Which was something the Grinch couldn't stand in the least!

And THEN
They'd do something
He liked least of all!
Every *Who* down in *Who*-ville, the tall and the small,
Would stand close together, with Christmas bells ringing.
They'd stand hand-in-hand. And the *Whos* would start singing!

They'd sing! *And they'd sing!*
AND they'd SING! SING! SING! SING!
And the more the Grinch thought of this *Who*-Christmas-Sing,
The more the Grinch thought, "I must stop this whole thing!
"Why, for fifty-three years I've put up with it now!
"I MUST stop this Christmas from coming!

         . . . But HOW?"

Then he got an idea!
An awful idea!
THE GRINCH
GOT A WONDERFUL, AWFUL IDEA!

"I know *just* what to do!" The Grinch laughed in his throat.
And he made a quick Santy Claus hat and a coat.
And he chuckled, and clucked, "What a great Grinchy trick!
"With this coat and this hat, I look just like Saint Nick!"

"All I need is a reindeer..."

The Grinch looked around.

But, since reindeer are scarce, there was none to be found.

Did that stop the old Grinch...?

No! The Grinch simply said,

"If I can't *find* a reindeer, I'll *make* one instead!"

So he called his dog, Max. Then he took some red thread

And he tied a big horn on the top of his head.

THEN

He loaded some bags
And some old empty sacks
On a ramshackle sleigh
And he hitched up old Max.

Then the Grinch said, "Giddap!"
And the sleigh started down
Toward the homes where the *Whos*
Lay a-snooze in their town.

All their windows were dark. Quiet snow filled the air.
All the *Whos* were all dreaming sweet dreams without care
When he came to the first little house on the square.
"This is stop number one," the old Grinchy Claus hissed
And he climbed to the roof, empty bags in his fist.

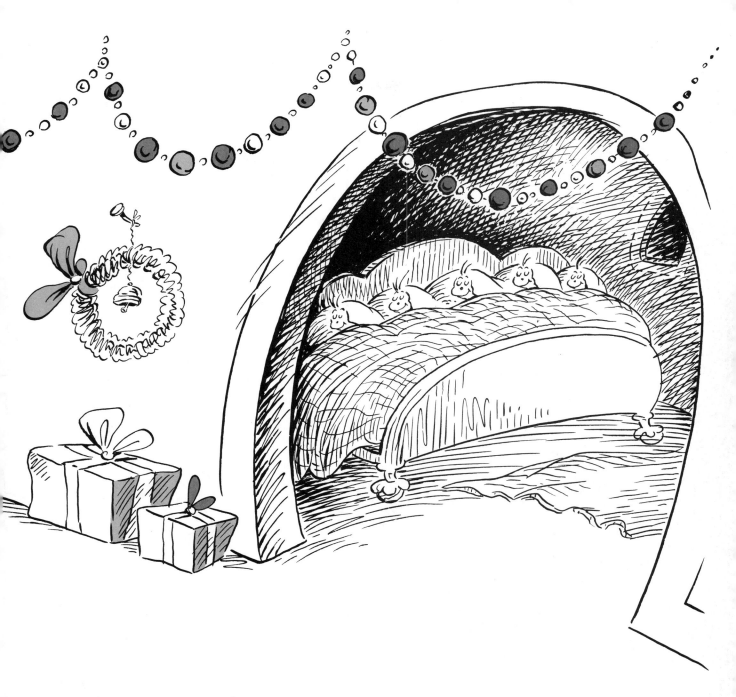

Then he slid down the chimney. A rather tight pinch.
But, if Santa could do it, then so could the Grinch.
He got stuck only once, for a moment or two.
Then he stuck his head out of the fireplace flue
Where the little *Who* stockings all hung in a row.
"These stockings," he grinned, "are the *first* things to go!"

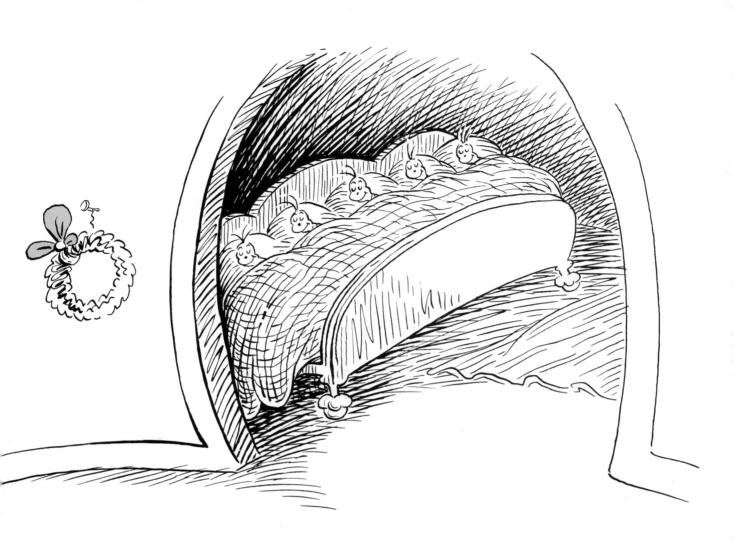

Then he slithered and slunk, with a smile most unpleasant,
Around the whole room, and he took every present!
Pop guns! And bicycles! Roller skates! Drums!
Checkerboards! Tricycles! Popcorn! And plums!
And he stuffed them in bags. Then the Grinch, very nimbly,
Stuffed all the bags, one by one, up the chimbley!

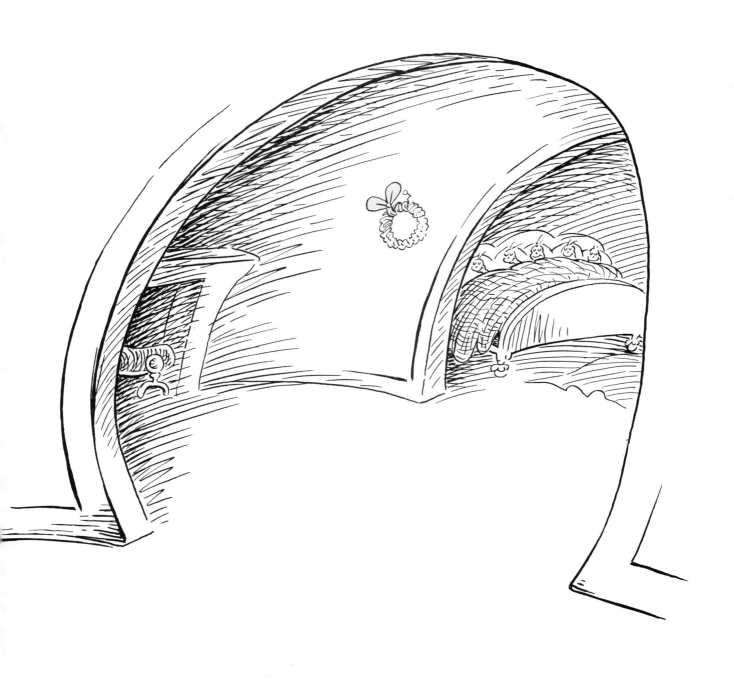

Then he slunk to the icebox. He took the *Whos'* feast!
He took the *Who*-pudding! He took the roast beast!
He cleaned out that icebox as quick as a flash.
Why, that Grinch even took their last can of *Who*-hash!

Then he stuffed all the food up the chimney with glee.
"And NOW!" grinned the Grinch, "I will stuff up the tree!"

And the Grinch grabbed the tree, and he started to shove
When he heard a small sound like the coo of a dove.
He turned around fast, and he saw a small *Who!*
Little Cindy-Lou *Who,* who was not more than two.

The Grinch had been caught by this tiny *Who* daughter
Who'd got out of bed for a cup of cold water.
She stared at the Grinch and said, "Santy Claus, why,
"*Why* are you taking our Christmas tree? WHY?"

But, you know, that old Grinch was so smart and so slick
He thought up a lie, and he thought it up quick!
"Why, my sweet little tot," the fake Santy Claus lied,
"There's a light on this tree that won't light on one side.
"So I'm taking it home to my workshop, my dear.
"I'll fix it up *there*. Then I'll bring it back *here*."

And his fib fooled the child. Then he patted her head
And he got her a drink and he sent her to bed.
And when Cindy-Lou *Who* went to bed with her cup,
HE went to the chimney and stuffed the tree up!

Then the *last* thing he took
Was the log for their fire!
Then he went up the chimney, himself, the old liar.
On their walls he left nothing but hooks and some wire.

And the one speck of food
That he left in the house
Was a crumb that was even too small for a mouse.

Then

He did the *same* thing
To the *other Whos'* houses

Leaving crumbs
Much too small
For the other *Whos'* mouses!

It was quarter past dawn . . .
    All the *Whos,* still a-bed,
    All the *Whos,* still a-snooze
When he packed up his sled,
Packed it up with their presents! The ribbons! The wrappings!
The tags! And the tinsel! The trimmings! The trappings!

Three thousand feet up! Up the side of Mt. Crumpit,
He rode with his load to the tiptop to dump it!
"Pooh-Pooh to the *Whos!*" he was grinch-ish-ly humming.
"They're finding out now that no Christmas is coming!
"They're just waking up! I know *just* what they'll do!
"Their mouths will hang open a minute or two
"Then the *Whos* down in *Who*-ville will all cry BOO-HOO!

"That's a noise," grinned the Grinch,
"That I simply MUST hear!"
So he paused. And the Grinch put his hand to his ear.
And he *did* hear a sound rising over the snow.
It started in low. Then it started to grow...

But the sound wasn't *sad!*
Why, this sound sounded *merry!*
It *couldn't* be so!
But it WAS merry! VERY!

He stared down at *Who*-ville!
The Grinch popped his eyes!
Then he shook!
What he saw was a shocking surprise!

Every *Who* down in *Who*-ville, the tall and the small,
Was singing! Without any presents at all!

He HADN'T stopped Christmas from coming!
IT CAME!
Somehow or other, it came just the same!

And the Grinch, with his grinch-feet ice-cold in the snow,
Stood puzzling and puzzling: "How *could* it be so?
"It came without ribbons! It came without tags!
"It came without packages, boxes or bags!"
And he puzzled three hours, till his puzzler was sore.
Then the Grinch thought of something he hadn't before!
"Maybe Christmas," he thought, *"doesn't* come from a store.
"Maybe Christmas . . . perhaps . . . means a little bit more!"

And what happened *then* . . . ?
Well . . . in *Who*-ville they say
That the Grinch's small heart
Grew three sizes that day!
And the minute his heart didn't feel quite so tight,
He whizzed with his load through the bright morning light
And he brought back the toys! And the food for the feast!
And he . . .

...HE HIMSELF...!
The Grinch carved the roast beast!

The LORAX

At the far end of town
where the Grickle-grass grows
and the wind smells slow-and-sour when it blows
and no birds ever sing excepting old crows...
is the Street of the Lifted Lorax.

And deep in the Grickle-grass, some people say,
if you look deep enough you can still see, today,
where the Lorax once stood
just as long as it could
before somebody lifted the Lorax away.

What *was* the Lorax?
And why was it there?
And why was it lifted and taken somewhere
from the far end of town where the Grickle-grass grows?
The old Once-ler still lives here.
Ask him. *He* knows.

You won't see the Once-ler.
Don't knock at his door.
He stays in his Lerkim on top of his store.
He lurks in his Lerkim, cold under the roof,
where he makes his own clothes
out of miff-muffered moof.
And on special dank midnights in August,
he peeks
out of the shutters
and sometimes he speaks
and tells how the Lorax was lifted away.

He'll tell you, perhaps...
if you're willing to pay.

On the end of a rope
he lets down a tin pail
and you have to toss in fifteen cents
and a nail
and the shell of a great-great-great-
grandfather snail.

Then he pulls up the pail,
makes a most careful count
to see if you've paid him
the proper amount.

Then he hides what you paid him
away in his Snuvv,
his secret strange hole
in his gruvvulous glove.

Then he grunts, "I will call you by Whisper-ma-Phone,
for the secrets I tell are for your ears alone."

SLUPP!
Down slupps the Whisper-ma-Phone to your ear
and the old Once-ler's whispers are not very clear,
since they have to come down
through a snergelly hose,
and he sounds
as if he had
smallish bees up his nose.

"Now I'll tell you," he says, with his teeth sounding gray,
"how the Lorax got lifted and taken away...

It all started way back...
such a long, long time back...

Way back in the days when the grass was still green
and the pond was still wet
and the clouds were still clean,
and the song of the Swomee-Swans rang out in space...
one morning, I came to this glorious place.
And I first saw the trees!
The Truffula Trees!
The bright-colored tufts of the Truffula Trees!
Mile after mile in the fresh morning breeze.

ONCE-LER
WAGON

And, under the trees, I saw Brown Bar-ba-loots
frisking about in their Bar-ba-loot suits
as they played in the shade and ate Truffula Fruits.

From the rippulous pond
came the comfortable sound
of the Humming-Fish humming
while splashing around.

But those *trees!* Those *trees!*
Those Truffula Trees!
All my life I'd been searching
for trees such as these.
The touch of their tufts
was much softer than silk.
And they had the sweet smell
of fresh butterfly milk.

I felt a great leaping
of joy in my heart.
I knew just what I'd do!
I unloaded my cart.

In no time at all, I had built a small shop.
Then I chopped down a Truffula Tree with one chop.
And with great skillful skill and with great speedy speed,
I took the soft tuft. And I knitted a Thneed!

The instant I'd finished, I heard a *ga-Zump!*
I looked.
I saw something pop out of the stump
of the tree I'd chopped down. It was sort of a man.
Describe him?...That's hard. I don't know if I can.

He was shortish. And oldish.
And brownish. And mossy.
And he spoke with a voice
that was sharpish and bossy.

"Mister!" he said with a sawdusty sneeze,
"I am the Lorax. I speak for the trees.
I speak for the trees, for the trees have no tongues.
And I'm asking you, sir, at the top of my lungs"—
he was very upset as he shouted and puffed—
"*What's that THING you've made out of my Truffula tuft?*"

"Look, Lorax," I said. "There's no cause for alarm.
I chopped just one tree. I am doing no harm.
I'm being quite useful. This thing is a Thneed.
A Thneed's a Fine-Something-That-All-People-Need!
It's a shirt. It's a sock. It's a glove. It's a hat.
But it has *other* uses. Yes, far beyond that.
You can use it for carpets. For pillows! For sheets!
Or curtains! Or covers for bicycle seats!"

The Lorax said,
"Sir! You are crazy with greed.
There is no one on earth
who would buy that fool Thneed!"

But the very next minute I proved he was wrong.
For, just at that minute, a chap came along,
and he thought that the Thneed I had knitted was great.
He happily bought it for three ninety-eight.

I laughed at the Lorax, "You poor stupid guy!
You never can tell what some people will buy."

"I repeat," cried the Lorax,
"I speak for the trees!"

"I'm busy," I told him.
"Shut up, if you please."

I rushed 'cross the room, and in no time at all,
built a radio-phone. I put in a quick call.
I called all my brothers and uncles and aunts
and I said, "Listen here! Here's a wonderful chance
for the whole Once-ler Family to get mighty rich!
Get over here fast! Take the road to North Nitch.
Turn left at Weehawken. Sharp right at South Stitch."

And, in no time at all,
in the factory I built,
the whole Once-ler Family
was working full tilt.
We were all knitting Thneeds
just as busy as bees,
to the sound of the chopping
of Truffula Trees.

314

Then...
Oh! Baby! Oh!
How my business did grow!
Now, chopping one tree
at a time
was too slow.

So I quickly invented my Super-Axe-Hacker
which whacked off four Truffula Trees at one smacker.
We were making Thneeds
four times as fast as before!
And that Lorax?...
He didn't show up any more.

But the next week
he knocked
on my new office door.

He snapped, "I'm the Lorax who speaks for the trees
which you seem to be chopping as fast as you please.
But I'm *also* in charge of the Brown Bar-ba-loots
who played in the shade in their Bar-ba-loot suits
and happily lived, eating Truffula Fruits.

"NOW...thanks to your hacking my trees to the ground,
there's not enough Truffula Fruit to go 'round.
And my poor Bar-ba-loots are all getting the crummies
because they have gas, and no food, in their tummies!

"They loved living here. But I can't let them stay.
They'll have to find food. And I hope that they may.
Good luck, boys," he cried. And he sent them away.

I, the Once-ler, felt sad
as I watched them all go.
BUT...
business is business!
And business must grow
regardless of crummies in tummies, you know.

I meant no harm. I most truly did not.
But I had to grow bigger. So bigger I got.
I biggered my factory. I biggered my roads.
I biggered my wagons. I biggered the loads
of the Thneeds I shipped out. I was shipping them forth
to the South! To the East! To the West! To the North!
I went right on biggering...selling more Thneeds.
And I biggered my money, which everyone needs.

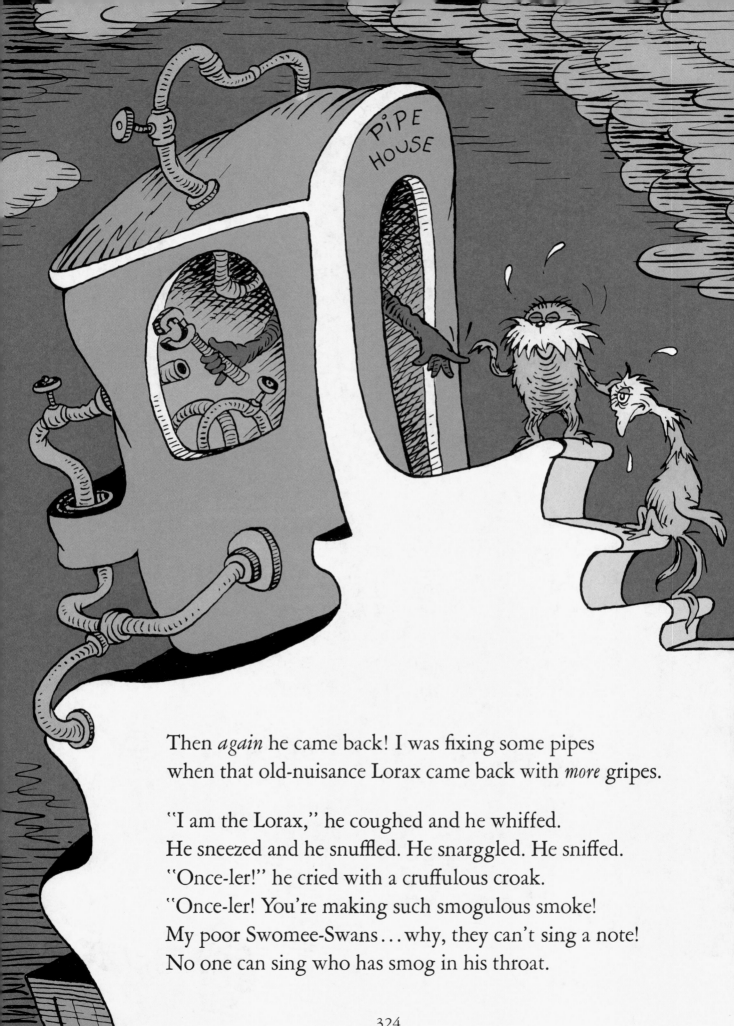

Then *again* he came back! I was fixing some pipes
when that old-nuisance Lorax came back with *more* gripes.

"I am the Lorax," he coughed and he whiffed.
He sneezed and he snuffled. He snarggled. He sniffed.
"Once-ler!" he cried with a cruffulous croak.
"Once-ler! You're making such smogulous smoke!
My poor Swomee-Swans...why, they can't sing a note!
No one can sing who has smog in his throat.

"And so," said the Lorax,
"—please pardon my cough—
they cannot live here.
So I'm sending them off.

"Where will they go?...
I don't hopefully know.

They may have to fly for a month...or a year...
To escape from the smog you've smogged-up around here.

"What's *more*," snapped the Lorax. (His dander was up.)
"Let me say a few words about Gluppity-Glupp.
Your machinery chugs on, day and night without stop
making Gluppity-Glupp. Also Schloppity-Schlopp.
And what do you do with this leftover goo?...
I'll show you. You dirty old Once-ler man, you!

"You're glumping the pond where the Humming-Fish hummed!
No more can they hum, for their gills are all gummed.
So I'm sending them off. Oh, their future is dreary.
They'll walk on their fins and get woefully weary
in search of some water that isn't so smeary."

And then I got mad.
I got terribly mad.
I yelled at the Lorax, "Now listen here, Dad!
All you do is yap-yap and say, 'Bad! Bad! Bad! Bad!'
Well, I have my rights, sir, and I'm telling *you*
I intend to go on doing just what I do!
And, for your information, you Lorax, I'm figgering
on biggering

    and BIGGERING

        and **BIGGERING**

           and **BIGGERING**,

turning MORE Truffula Trees into Thneeds
which everyone, EVERYONE, *EVERYONE* needs!"

And at that very moment, we heard a loud whack!
From outside in the fields came a sickening smack
of an axe on a tree. Then we heard the tree fall.
The very last Truffula Tree of them all!

No more trees. No more Thneeds. No more work to be done.
So, in no time, my uncles and aunts, every one,
all waved me good-bye. They jumped into my cars
and drove away under the smoke-smuggered stars.

Now all that was left 'neath the bad-smelling sky
was my big empty factory...
the Lorax...
and I.

The Lorax said nothing. Just gave me a glance...
just gave me a very sad, sad backward glance...
as he lifted himself by the seat of his pants.
And I'll never forget the grim look on his face
when he heisted himself and took leave of this place,
through a hole in the smog, without leaving a trace.

And all that the Lorax left here in this mess
was a small pile of rocks, with the one word...
"UNLESS."
Whatever *that* meant, well, I just couldn't guess.

That was long, long ago.
But each day since that day
I've sat here and worried
and worried away.
Through the years, while my buildings
have fallen apart,
I've worried about it
with all of my heart.

"But *now*," says the Once-ler,
"Now that *you're* here,
the word of the Lorax seems perfectly clear.
UNLESS someone like you
cares a whole awful lot,
nothing is going to get better.
It's not.

"SO...
Catch!" calls the Once-ler.
He lets something fall.
"It's a Truffula Seed.
It's the last one of all!
You're in charge of the last of the Truffula Seeds.
And Truffula Trees are what everyone needs.
Plant a new Truffula. Treat it with care.
Give it clean water. And feed it fresh air.
Grow a forest. Protect it from axes that hack.
Then the Lorax
and all of his friends
may come back."

THEODOR SEUSS GEISEL, known to his millions of fans as Dr. Seuss, wrote and illustrated forty-four books. He forever changed the face of children's literature in 1937 with his first book, *And to Think That I Saw It on Mulberry Street.* His last, *Oh, the Places You'll Go!,* was on the *New York Times* bestseller list for over two years. He was credited with bringing fun into the process of learning to read after he launched Beginner Books with *The Cat in the Hat* in 1957.

Long considered a national treasure, Dr. Seuss was awarded a Pulitzer Prize Special Citation in 1984. He received virtually every children's book award, including the Laura Ingalls Wilder Medal and three Caldecott Honors for *McElligot's Pool, Bartholomew and the Oobleck,* and *If I Ran the Zoo.* In addition, works based on his original stories have won three Oscars, three Emmys, three Grammys, and a Peabody Award.

Dr. Seuss was born in Springfield, Massachusetts, on March 2, 1904, and died at his home in La Jolla, California, on September 24, 1991.

Books written and illustrated by Dr. Seuss:

AND TO THINK THAT I SAW IT ON MULBERRY STREET
THE 500 HATS OF BARTHOLOMEW CUBBINS
THE SEVEN LADY GODIVAS
THE KING'S STILTS
HORTON HATCHES THE EGG
McELLIGOT'S POOL
THIDWICK THE BIG-HEARTED MOOSE
BARTHOLOMEW AND THE OOBLECK
IF I RAN THE ZOO
SCRAMBLED EGGS SUPER!
HORTON HEARS A WHO!
ON BEYOND ZEBRA!
IF I RAN THE CIRCUS
HOW THE GRINCH STOLE CHRISTMAS!
YERTLE THE TURTLE AND OTHER STORIES
HAPPY BIRTHDAY TO YOU!
THE SNEETCHES AND OTHER STORIES
DR. SEUSS'S SLEEP BOOK
I HAD TROUBLE IN GETTING TO SOLLA SOLLEW
THE CAT IN THE HAT SONGBOOK
I CAN LICK 30 TIGERS TODAY! AND OTHER STORIES
I CAN DRAW IT MYSELF
THE LORAX
DID I EVER TELL YOU HOW LUCKY YOU ARE?
HUNCHES IN BUNCHES
THE BUTTER BATTLE BOOK
YOU'RE ONLY OLD ONCE!
OH, THE PLACES YOU'LL GO!

Beginner Books
THE CAT IN THE HAT
THE CAT IN THE HAT COMES BACK
ONE FISH TWO FISH RED FISH BLUE FISH
GREEN EGGS AND HAM
HOP ON POP
DR. SEUSS'S ABC
FOX IN SOCKS
THE FOOT BOOK
MR. BROWN CAN MOO! CAN YOU?
MARVIN K. MOONEY WILL YOU PLEASE GO NOW!
THE SHAPE OF ME AND OTHER STUFF
THERE'S A WOCKET IN MY POCKET!
OH, THE THINKS YOU CAN THINK!
THE CAT'S QUIZZER
I CAN READ WITH MY EYES SHUT!
OH SAY CAN YOU SAY?